Karma's WORLD

VIRAL VIDEO SHOWDOWN

BY JEHAN MADHANI

SCHOLASTIC INC.

FOR MUSY AND FOR SERENE
(WHO IS TOO NEW TO HAVE A NICKNAME)

CHAPTER 1

"Go, Karma, go, Karma, go, Karma!" There's nothing like hearing a crowd cheering your name . . . especially when that crowd is made up of your best friends! Winston and Switch were my two best friends in the world, and they were cheering me on as I danced my heart out on my front stoop.

I loved to rap and dance, but as much as I loved the spotlight and performing for an

audience, sometimes it's even more fun to just jam with your friends. And I was *feeling* this beat.

"Karma, these moves are next level!" Winston shouted over the music, waving his hands above his head like he was at a concert. Winston Torres has been my best friend since we were in diapers. He's been cheering me on since before we could even speak in full sentences. Rumor has it that "Go, Karma" might have been his first words. That, or "Action!" since he's been directing me in his movies and music videos for just as long.

I don't wanna brag, but I had to admit, Winston was right. My feet had really caught this beat, and these moves were definitely next level. I smiled big back at Winston as I threw in another slide and rolled my shoulders with the music, which was *also* next level. This beat was bumpin'!

"Ooooooh, Switch! Don't stop that beat!" I called out to my other best friend, Switch. Switch Stein has been our best friend ever since she moved to Hansberry Heights with her mom at the start of this school year. We didn't even know her last year, but now me and Winston couldn't have imagined the fifth grade without her. The three of us do everything together, and we always have one another's backs. She loves music just like we do! And she is a *fire* music producer. In fact, she made the beat that was blasting out of the speakers on her backpack. Pretty incredible, huh?

"You got it, Karm!" Switch smiled and increased the volume on her backpack speakers. This beat was her best one yet. (I say that about all of them, but it's true!) It was a fun, bouncy hip-hop beat that made you want to move your feet, and when Switch hit play, I couldn't help but start dancing. The song was like total dance magic.

Switch and I first realized we loved dancing together when we auditioned for the In-Step Squad, Hansberry Height's elite dance squad. When Carrie Bautista didn't let Switch on the squad even though she was *definitely* the best dancer who auditioned, I decided I didn't want to be on a team like that. Switch and I might not have made the In-Step Squad, but we knew that the two of us *had* to keep dancing together. That's when we started our own dance crew, the Full Out Dance Crew. Our friends

Megan, Mateo, Chris, and even my dog, Major, are also on the crew. And when we dance together, we dance *full out*. Dancing full out means you dance with your whole heart. Switch taught me that!

"Woo-hoo! Goooo, Karma . . . you're dancing full out!" Switch called to me from next to Winston, clapping excitedly as I jumped up and down. I grinned at her. She was right. I closed my eyes and swiveled my hips with the beat. By the time the song was over, I had made a whole dance routine!

As the beat faded, I ended with a big finale and finished leaning with my arms crossed. Winston and Switch both leapt to their feet to give me a standing ovation. Like I said, they're *the best*.

"Karma, that dance was *soooo* cool." Winston tried to do the slide I did during the chorus, wiggling his arms. He's not very good at dancing, but he totally tries.

"You know, I think it might be the best dance I've ever made . . . but I couldn't have done it without that beat. It was totally poppin', Switch! It really made me want to move . . . it was like total dance magic!" Switch blushed.

"Thanks, Karm. I looooved your dance. I gotta try some of those moves. Will you teach me?" Switch asked as she started to do the arm motion from the end of my dance.

"Of course! But you can't learn it down there! Get up here!" I ran over and held out my hand to Switch, pulling her up to stand next to me on the stoop. Dancing with Switch was pretty high on my list of favorite things to do ever, so of course I was gonna show her how to do my new dance. Winston hit play on the backpack speakers, and Switch and I stood side by side.

"So first you cross your fists across your body like you're hitting your hips," I told Switch. She watched closely and quickly did the same move.

"And then when this part of the song comes, you want to sliiiiide!" I slid across the stoop real smooth, and Switch followed me.

"And you clap above your right leg, then you lift your leg and clap under it this time."

Switch followed along.

"And then you spiiiin all the way around. And end big with a shoulder roll like this!"

Switch did it just like I had.

"Yes! Exactly like that. You're doing it!" Before I knew it, Switch had the whole dance down. That didn't surprise me—Switch is the best dancer I know. She's also a totally amazing choreographer. She was usually the one who came up with the dances for our Full Out squad. She has an amazing talent for mixing all our different moves—from my steps to Mateo and Megan's ballroom twirls—to make something even more incredible that felt like all of us! She makes pretty much any dance she does better.

When we finished doing the dance again,

I was exhausted! I took a deep breath and wiped the sweat off my forehead. I grabbed my water bottle and took a biiiig sip.

"Phew . . . I need a sip of water—all this dancing has me sweating!" It was a pretty warm spring day, and I was finally starting to feel a little tired from all that dancing. I was excited to take a breather and lean against the stoop. And luckily, Switch was still movin'. I was happy to watch her do her thing. I hit the play button on the speakers one more time so she could keep going.

Switch started to dance. She was totally getting it!

"This dance is totally, completely incredible!" Winston told me with a smile. I agreed. Suddenly, Winston put his hand to his forehead, shaking his head in realization.

"Wait . . . this dance *is* totally, completely incredible! I should be filming this! *Why* am I not filming this? I gotta be filming this!" Winston shook his head at himself in disbelief. Winston is a really talented artist, and he loves filming and directing music videos. Sometimes when he gets an idea for a project, his energy comes bursting out all at once and he can't help it. This was definitely one of those times. Winston jumped up off our step, excited to capture the dance on camera. He almost tripped over himself running to get the camera from his bag at the bottom of the stairs. CRASH. Down he goes.

"I'm okay!" He shakily held up his camera with a sheepish grin. Winston could be a little clumsy. He laughed as he held up his camera. "That's why I leave the dancing to you two!" Switch and I couldn't stop laughing.

As Switch did my dance, Winston started film-ing and quickly went into full Winston director mode, carefully moving around and trying to keep the camera steady.

I giggled as I watched Winston crouch and

stretch and move his long legs and arms into different twisted-up positions to get the camera angles he wanted. He stuck his tongue out in concentration. He looked a little bit like a pretzel.

I leaned over to turn up the volume on Switch's backpack. We were gonna need the music playing loud and clear in that video.

I nodded and clapped along as Switch did the moves. When Switch hit the final shoulder roll, I jumped up, clapping enthusiastically—it was my turn to give my besties a standing ovation. Only, Switch wasn't done! She kept going, whipping her arm around in a big circle, ending with a big drop almost to the ground! Whoa. Cool.

"Switch, the dance looked soooo good! And, Winston, that was some uh-mazing cool camera work!" I ran over to throw my arms around both of them for a group hug. "Switch, I loved that move at the end!"

"Thanks! I call it Switch's Arm Swing Thing." As she said each word, Switch did one of the motions—first the arm up, then a big swing in a circle, and then she dropped down into the split. I giggled and helped her up. We turned to the tablet impatiently. We had to see what the video looked like!

"What's it look like, Winnie? Let me see, let me see!" He hurriedly flipped out the video camera's screen so I could look, too, and pressed

★ ‖ ★

play. A scratchier version of the song started playing as the recording of Switch dancing started. It looked even better than I had imagined.

"Whoaaaa." We all had to admit, that dance video was something else! Winston had done a great job filming and capturing all the moves, and Switch had taken my dance and given it lots of her own special Switch flair with her Arm Swing Thing. While we were watching, Switch started to get more and more excited.

"Wait . . . Oh my gosh . . . I just had a totally, completely amazing idea. What if I post the video and song to MyBlock?! And then other people could learn it . . . and then they could post their versions, and then other people would see it and post their versions, and then . . . and then and it could be like a new neighborhood dance challenge!" Switch took a deep breath. When she gets super excited about something, she talks really fast. Like, really fast.

"That sounds like the best idea I've ever heard!" Winston exclaimed.

"Yeah, let's do it!" I agreed with Winston—it was a pretty cool idea! Switch smiled big and pulled up MyBlock on her phone, and we all gathered around as Winston shared the video with her from his camera. MyBlock is the social media platform in our neighborhood. Everyone used it to share their family updates and neighborhood news with the rest of Hansberry Heights, and it let us show our neighbors the latest cool trends. Switch picked up her phone and started uploading.

"Okay . . . I added a caption about the challenge, and now it's uploading . . . could it be any slower?" Switch sighed. We watched the progress bar slowly move as the video file uploaded. I looked over her shoulder and saw the video's title. I read it out loud.

"'Switch It Up with the Switch Stein Switch' . . ." The video title made me feel a little funny, but when she heard me read it, Switch just smiled even bigger.

"Yeah! I thought of calling the dance the Switch Stein Switch . . . Because I'm Switch, and I switch it up in the video!" Switch giggled when she said that and did a little shimmy. "And then I thought that was the perfect video title to get everyone to click!" Switch seemed so excited that I didn't really want to say anything about the name of the dance. We all kept looking at the screen, waiting for the upload to finish.

"Looks like Mr. Singal posted another new turtle lullaby." Winston pointed to a video of our teacher, Mr. Singal, singing to his pet turtle, Cuebert. Cuebert did not look that interested.

"Phew . . . well, it looks like it'll put Cuebert right to sleep." We giggled at the video. Then we heard a DING. It was a MyBlock notification.

"It's done, it's done!" Switch was hopping up and down. We all crowded around the phone. Yup, sure enough, the video was up! It had zero views. But I was sure that wouldn't be the case for long! We all sat looking at the phone for a while longer, but nothing happened. Maybe I was wrong about all those views. The longer we looked, the less sure I was. I shrugged.

"I guess now . . . we wait?"

CHAPTER 2

The next morning, I was feeling a little better about the name of the dance. In fact, I was barely even thinking about it. Maybe it wasn't that big of a deal. After all, when I went to bed, nobody had even looked at it yet! *Maybe* it didn't even matter that Switch put her name on the dance even though I was the one who thought it up. Ugh. I guess I *was* still thinking about it a little. And I was definitely more than a little frustrated!

But soon I had way more important things to think about than the dance! Because when I went downstairs for breakfast, I heard the coolest news ever on *Good Morning Brenda*.

Good Morning Brenda is our local Hansberry Heights morning news show. Brenda's on top of everything Hansberry. That was actually her catchphrase: "I'm Brenda, and I'm on Top of Everything Hansberry!" If I had written it, I probably would have made it rhyme, but it was still pretty catchy. And when you hear that classic Brenda catchphrase, you know you're gonna hear the latest Hansberry scoop! Sometimes my family liked to turn on Brenda's show in the mornings with breakfast to hear what's up! I didn't always pay attention, but this morning, she was totally, completely, speaking my language.

"Tune in when we come back from commercial to hear all about an exciting new opportunity for young Hansberry musicians!" I perked up when I heard that. An opportunity for young Hansberry musicians? I wondered what it could be.

I rushed to finish pouring my cereal so I could sit at the table with Mom, Dad, and my little brother, Keys. Mom and Dad were each reading a section of the newspaper, and Keys was elbows-deep in his latest and greatest invention. It looked like it used to be his electric scooter . . . but he had added a whole bunch of buttons and gadgets to it. He had attached one of Dad's music stands to it with a whole lot of tape and put his math workbook on it. Keys is always making something totally cool, and usually it's also the teensiest bit dangerous. The scooter kept beeping like it was on the fritz. This was pretty normal for a morning at the Grant breakfast table. And it was time for me to liven it up a little!

"Good mooooorning!" I sang.

"Mooooorning, Kar-Star!" My dad yawned as he sang back to me. He reached over and pulled me into a hug. Mom and Dad weren't tooooootally awake yet.

"Karma, I can barely hear the capacitator on my homework decombobulator over all that noise!" I didn't know how many of the words Keys said were real, but his scooter spat out a cloud of smoke, so something was definitely happening in there.

"The what?"

"The homework decombobulator. It's part of my new Scoot-N-Study! Soon I'll be able to do my homework on the go. Part desk, part scooter, *all* business!"

The *Good Morning Brenda* music started to play on the TV. "And now back to *Good Morning Brenda*!"

"Keys, shhhhh! Brenda said she had a cool announcement! For musicians!" I went back to focusing on Brenda, and I was glad I did, because it seemed almost like she was talking directly to me.

"Is there a young hip-hop fan in your life?"

"Uh . . . yeah." Young hip-hop fan? I thought that I fit that description pretty perfectly.

"Are they trying to perfect their musical craft?"

"Uh . . . double yeah?" My eyes widened. I looked at Mom and Dad, but they were still enjoying their breakfast. Mom and Dad were usually pretty tired before they finished their coffee, so instead, I decided to get the attention of someone who doesn't need *any* coffee to have energy in the morning.

"Keys, are you hearing this?" Keys waved a wrench at me.

"All I'm hearing is you talking while I'm trying to get the Scoot-N-Study up and running." I shook my head at him and turned back to focus on Brenda.

"Well, if you know a young hip-hop fan who

wants to pick up the latest, most cutting-edge moves, then Camp Rhyme is for you! This spring's citywide hip-hop sleepaway camp experience is like nothing you've ever seen!" I gasped. I had to go.

"Kids will have the opportunity to learn every-thing about hip-hop—rapping, dancing, making beats, and more! All while surrounded by fellow campers and counselors who love making music."

"Mom, Dad, did you hear that? There's a whole spring break camp for kids like me who love hip-hop and want to be rappers!" I leaned across the table to get their attention and waved my hand dramatically at the TV. This was more important than their morning coffee and the newspaper! This was about their favorite and only daughter's future!

"That *does* sound perfect for you," Mom said.

Yes! Even my mom thought it was perfect for me. That seemed like a good sign that I'd get to go. I was practically jumping up and down I was so excited.

"That sounds amazing, Kar-Star!" And my dad agreed with her! This camp seemed like a definite yes now that I had both of them on board. This time I really did jump up and down! This was the best news ever.

But then . . . Dad kept talking. "Let's look into it first. A specialized camp like that could be pretty expensive." Oh . . . so maybe it wasn't a total yes yet.

"Okay . . ." I didn't mean to sound so disappointed, but I *was* disappointed. This camp sounded like a dream come true. My mom ran a hand through my hair like she does when I get upset.

"It does sound like a wonderful opportunity, but you're also doing such a great job learning all about hip-hop right here at home, Karma." My mom did usually know exactly what to say to make me feel better.

My dad nodded in agreement. "Kar-Star, you probably know more about hip-hop and rapping than the counselors at that camp. You're a rap expert! How many other kids can say they personally know  Lady K *and* can rap every MC Grillz rhyme there is?"

My parents were right, but I still really, really wanted to go to this camp. I'd get to meet other kids like me who lived and breathed hip-hop! It was the perfect place for me.

"I guess that's true. But it would be next level if I could go to the camp."

"We'll think about it, Kar-Star." My mom smiled at me. It wasn't a no, but it also wasn't a yes. I went back to my cereal, and before I had even finished my next bite, I had already decided that I had to figure out a way to get to that camp. I took another big bite of cereal as I tried to come up with a plan to get there. But I couldn't focus on my planning for very long because suddenly Keys was shouting right in my ear.

"Turn it up, turn it up! They're talking about Switch!" I almost spit out my cereal! They're talking about Switch . . . on TV?

"Sthey're wha?" I said with my mouth full. I chewed and swallowed and tried again. "They're what?!" I must have misheard Keys. I would have known if my best friend was gonna be talked about on the news!

"They're talking about Switch!" This time it was my mom who repeated what Keys said as she turned the volume up on the TV.

"That's right! There's a new dance sensation taking over Hansberry Heights!" Uh . . . did I hear that right? "It's called the Switch Stein Switch. The newest MyBlock dance challenge by our very own Switch Stein! And that's not all! The video, uploaded last night, has caught the attention of our community and has gotten everyone up, active, and grooving! You can see neighbors all over Hansberry Heights learning the moves and putting their own spin on this viral vid."

"Viral? But nobody had even watched it when we went to bed last night!" I couldn't believe my ears. But Brenda had started airing clips of . . . everyone doing the dance! Ms. Washington . . . Tommie . . . Sam . . . Even Ms. Mortimer the art teacher!

"Uh . . . I guess a lot of people were dancing

after your bedtime, Karma. Because this video has thousands of views." Keys pulled up the video from MyBlock on his tablet. As we looked at it, even more comments showed up. People were really, *really* loving this dance. There was Ms. Torres, and Auggie . . . it seemed like the whole neighborhood was online this morning to tell Switch how much they loved her moves.

Keys started to read the comments out loud as he scrolled through them. "There's a lot of comments! And they all love Switch! 'This dance is sooo fun! Way to go, Switch!' 'Switch, your moves are pure poetry!' 'I love switchin' up the Switch Stein Switch! Bet you can't say that five times fast!' Oh yes, I bet I can! Switchin' up the swish shtein swish. Swishin up the swish! Siwishin. Arrrrgh! Switch Stein Swish. Noooo!" It sounded like Keys was going to be doing that for a while, but I couldn't even giggle at his silliness like normal.

Everybody was loving the Switch Stein

Switch, and nobody knew I had done the dance first. My stomach dropped, and suddenly my cereal felt like mush in my mouth. I guess Switch did add the Arm Swing Thing, but something just didn't feel right. I totally zoned out as I ate the rest of my cereal, until Keys shouted right in my ear again. He needed to invent me some Keys Grant patented earplugs with all this shouting.

"Karma, it's time to go or we're gonna be laaaate!" Keys had carefully packed up his invention and started pushing me out of my chair. I stood up and grabbed my backpack, ready to go, but then I slowed down. We always walked to school with Switch and Winston, and this morning . . . I wasn't as excited to see them as I normally was. But Keys put his hands on my backpack and pushed.

"Karmaaaa, let's go! Winston and Switch are already here, and I wanna ask them all about the Swish Shtein Swich. Awww man, now I can't say it at all! Switch. Switch. Switch Swischh."

I sighed and dragged my feet to the door. As soon as I stepped onto the stoop, Winston and Switch were suddenly in my face, both talking over each other, super excited about their hit video.

"Karma, did you see how many views my dance has?" As I walked down the steps, Switch hugged me, she was so excited.

"Karma, Switch is going viral. With a video I took! I can't believe it! Do I need an agent? Should I get an agent?" Winston said.

"Yeah . . . we saw it on *Good Morning Brenda*. That's really cool." I tried to be supportive, but I didn't really know what to say. Luckily for me, Keys always had a lot to say.

"And after we saw the *Brenda* segment, we went and read all the comments on MyBlock! People loooove the Swish Ssstein Swish . . . It's a little hard to say, though."

Winston and Switch both giggled. Keys then

started trying to do the dance, making them laugh even harder. He clapped his hands above his leg and then did a silly wiggle instead of the roll at the end. Even I cracked a smiled. My little brother is a *terrible* dancer.

"This is the most views anything on my MyBlock page has ever gotten!" Switch was so  excited. She was waving her phone around. PING—PING—PING. It was getting notifications nonstop. "It hasn't stopped going off all morning. Everyone is sharing and commenting on it!"

I tried to keep smiling, but my heart wasn't really in it. I still wasn't sure how I felt. But I really, really wanted to be happy that my friends were so excited.

♪ ♫ ♪

I couldn't even put the dance out of my mind on the way to school because suddenly everybody was doing it. And I mean *everybody*.

First, we passed my downstairs neighbor Mr. Crawford trying to get it right on the beat. When he saw us, he called out to Switch.

"Hey, Switch . . . how do you do that hop to the left?" Mr. Crawford is always grumpy. And now even he was hopping to Switch's beat! But *I* was the one who taught Switch that hop. And it didn't stop there. It felt like everywhere we went someone was learning the Switch Stein Switch or shouting out Switch's moves. Ms. Washington, Chef Scott . . . they were all hopping and bopping and doing the Switch Stein Switch. For once, I was more excited to focus on school than on dancing. But it turned out . . . things were even worse at school.

CHAPTER 3

When Winston, Switch, and I entered the halls of Peach Tree Middle School that morning, it was like Winston and I walked in with a celebrity! Everyone wanted a chance to talk to Switch about her dance . . . Chris, Crash, Mateo, Sabiya. All our friends were congratulating Switch . . . . and kids we didn't even know were giving her high fives! She was so surprised by all the attention that she was blushing. Everyone at school loved the dance so much that it was all they could talk about. Demi Ray ran up to us.

"Switch . . . that dance is so amazing and was so much fun to learn. You're like . . . the dance queen of Peach Tree Middle." Demi Ray had a point. Switch *was* the best dancer in school.

"Ha-ha, don't let Carrie hear you say that!" Winston warned jokingly. He was right. Carrie Bautista definitely thought she was the best dancer in the school, and she wasn't very nice about competition. And worst of all . . . she was coming right toward us.

"Do you think she heard you?" I whispered to Winston. His eyebrows were raised, and he shrugged nervously. Switch and Demi Ray looked worried, too. We all held our breath. Carrie usually didn't have anything nice to say to us.

"Maybe she's just walking past us?" Winston said hopefully. Nope . . . she was coming straight to us. Carrie walked up with a flick of her long ponytail. She was in her In-Step

Dance Squad team uniform, like usual.

"Uh . . . hi, Carrie!" Winston's voice was just a squeak.

Carrie looked at him for a second, but she wasn't interested in talking to Winston.

"Um . . . hi. Anyway." Carrie turned and looked at Switch. "So, y'know . . . Switch . . . your new dance is totally cool. I'm going to do my version and post it to MyBlock this afternoon. Maybe you could give it a like? Or . . . maybe even comment on it? Mm . . . 'kay, thanks, bye!" As fast as she had arrived, Carrie left with another swish of her long ponytail. The whole conversation happened so fast that I thought I might have dreamt it.

"Oh . . . um . . . uh . . . thank you, Carrie!"

I wasn't the only shocked one. When Demi Ray, Winston, Switch, and I walked away from Carrie, our jaws dropped. Winston shook his head in amazement. "Switch . . . your dance is so good it turned Carrie nice for . . . a whole ten seconds! That's some real dance magic."

Winston and Switch giggled, and I tried to join them. Switch was normally behind the scenes making beats, so not everybody at school knew she was basically the coolest girl in our grade. And now everyone was seeing her the way Winston and I did. I had to admit . . . it was nice to see people recognize exactly how cool she was. But a not-so-little part of me still wished all the attention she was getting wasn't for *my* dance moves.

That whole day, it felt like the Switch Stein Switch was following me everywhere I went. Everyone was trying to do their best version. Chris and Mateo were trying to learn it in the art classroom, Sabiya was teaching Megan in the hallway, and even our teacher Mr. Singal talked about it during homeroom.

"Class, can you believe it? Peach Tree Middle's very own Switch Stein is an internet dance sensation! And she's in *my* homeroom. I'm starstruck. Cuebert, are you starstruck? We're all starstruck!" Mr. Singal's turtle, Cuebert, didn't look all that starstruck. In fact, he looked how I felt ... a little tired of hearing about this dance.

"Switch, why don't you tell the class all about how you created your dance?" Mr. Singal gestured for Switch to go up to the front of the class. Switch was a little nervous to talk in front of everyone at first.

"Thank you, Mr. Singal! Um ... This dance is ..."

Switch paused for a second, like she wasn't sure what to say next, and then Crash shouted, "Totally awesome!" The whole homeroom cheered in agreement. "Your moves are fire, Switch!" Crash loved rapping and performing as much as I did, and he was really competitive, so I was a little surprised to hear him give Switch her shine. He had a pretty big head, so this was a pretty big deal. Once Switch heard how much everybody, including Crash, liked the song, she started talking way faster.

"I'm so glad everyone likes the dance! I really, really love dancing. It's soooo much fun to get up and move. And I'm mostly just excited to get to share my dance with all of you, and with all my friends in Hansberry Heights!" Switch smiled big as she talked about how much she loved dance. When she talked about dance, she lit up, like I did when I talked about rapping. "It's so cool to see everyone as excited about dancing as I am!"

I stayed in Mr. Singal's empty classroom for a little bit before joining my friends for lunch. It was just me and Cuebert. Sometimes, when I have a lot to think about, it helps to write it down in my journal. Writing my thoughts down as lyrics has always helped me understand how I'm feeling. And since I still couldn't stop thinking about how Switch had taken credit for my moves, I decided to write it out. I took out my pen and my journal . . . and I started to write.

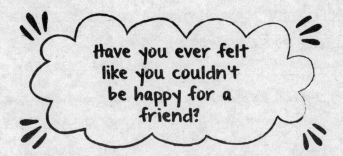

Have you ever felt like you couldn't be happy for a friend?

When Mr. Singal asked how she created the dance, Switch didn't even mention me, even though I did the dance first. That hurt. I was torn. I felt like I should be happy that my friend was being celebrated for doing the thing she loved most. So why do I feel so mad about her taking credit?

I love Switch and I want to be happy about her success, but what I really wish is that she had gotten all this attention for a dance she had made up on her own. She didn't create the dance. I did. The Switch Stein Switch was my dance first. I'm not sure how I'm supposed to feel. I want to be happy for her, but something doesn't feel right.

♫ I want to be happy for Switch and smile for real . . .

But it doesn't change how upset I feel

Those dance moves she's doing—they're awesome, they're fierce!

But I can't shake the feeling that they're not just hers!

I love that everybody is dancing and groovin'

It's amazing that this dance has our town up and movin'

But something about those moves doesn't feel great

Switch put her name on dance moves I helped originate

But Switch loves dancing . . . she's doing her dance thing

And I've seen firsthand the joy she brings

Switch is my bestie. I love seeing her shine

So I guess . . . maybe . . . I can try to be fine? ♪ ♪

Maybe it's okay to let Switch shine this time?

I sighed and closed my journal. I still wasn't totally happy, but I could try to be happy for Switch. I was usually center stage, taking the spotlight. And dancing really was Switch's thing. I went to the cafeteria to join my friends. When I got there, Switch and Winston were at our usual lunch table, surrounded by a crowd.

"Karma! There you are! Where have you been? Switch has been telling us more about the Switch Stein Switch!" Winston made room for me in my normal seat and waved me over. Why was I not surprised?

"Oh . . . cool! That's really great." I pushed my way past the crowd to take my seat at a table nearby. Switch wasn't even sitting in her normal seat. She was sitting high up on the table so the whole crowd could see her. It seemed like she was finally getting used to the attention. Sabiya and Megan were holding their phones shyly.

"Megan and I had so much fun making our

own version of the Switch Stein Switch ... would you maybe watch it? Let us know how we did? We'd really appreciate your expert opinion!" Sabiya held up the phone.

"Of course! I'd be happy to!" Switch took the phone happily and pressed play. I heard Switch's fire beat start up again. Everyone at the table started bopping their heads up and down. I had been so excited to play the song on repeat yesterday . . . but today I was all played out.

Sabiya and Megan smiled nervously and held hands while Switch watched the video. She finished watching and smiled. They sighed in relief.

"That was really great. I loved that little snap you added to the slide!" Switch did the snap and Sabiya smiled proudly.

"That was Megan's idea. I thought it was sooo cool. Not that the dance wasn't already cool. It's the coolest. Everybody loves it."

"Yeah! Switch, how did you even come up with such a cool dance?" Megan asked.

I held my breath. Maybe now Switch would finally talk about how I made the dance first?

"I can't even believe everyone loves it so much! It's just a dance I came up with on Karma's stoop!" When she said that, suddenly it was like I couldn't stop the words from coming out of my mouth.

"Except you didn't even make up the dance!"

Everyone at the table gasped. They looked at

me, and then back at Switch, like we were in a tennis match. Switch looked really hurt.

"Uh … Karma, the Switch Stein Switch is totally mine. I did, too, make it up."

"No, you didn't! They were my moves first. I made up the dance, and then I showed you the steps. I came up with the hop and the clapping, and the slide."

When I said that, everyone looked at Switch for an explanation. I crossed my arms. Maybe I shouldn't have accused Switch in front of everyone, but now that it was out in the open, I was glad. At least now Switch would have to give me credit and set the record straight.

"I added to it and made it mine." It was my turn to look hurt. My eyes were wide. "I made it better. And *that's* the dance everyone wants to do."

"Well, it's not *your* dance," I insisted. Switch and I both stood up.

"Yes, it is."

"No, it's not! You added one move." I looked around. Everyone was still watching. Switch sure didn't feel like my bestie.

"Winston, you were there! You saw me do the dance first."

"He saw *me* make the Switch Stein Switch!"

"Uh, Karma, Switch, maybe if you just—" Winston tried to help, but neither of us wanted to hear it.

"See you, Winston." Switch left in a huff.

"Yeah, see you." I grabbed my journal and started to walk out in the opposite direction.

Winston followed me. "Karma, I know you did the first version of the dance—"

It was nice to hear it from someone else who was there. But he didn't speak up when I needed him to.

"I'm not the one you should be saying that to, Winston. Everyone else thinks it's Switch's dance." Why wasn't anyone seeing this from my side?

CHAPTER 4

That afternoon, I stomped all the way home and *tried* to stomp all the way up into my room. But I couldn't because Keys was in front of the stairs trying to teach Major, our dog, the Switch Stein Switch. That dance was *everywhere*.

"Major, this is your ticket to the dance challenge big leagues! When everyone sees you wiggling that tail . . . you'll be the next big MyBlock star!"

Keys was coaching Major through the dance, and I had to admit, our puppy had moves. He was standing on his two hind legs and doing the slide with the cutest little tail wiggle. Keys kept coaching him.

"You're doing amazing! Now to the left! And do the Switch Stein Switch! Uh huh, uh huh." But even that couldn't help my bad mood. I couldn't stop thinking about how the dance wasn't even Switch's!

"Ughhhhhhh!" I let out a groan when I saw the dance. I stomped past Keys and Major. Keys shrugged, and Major kept dancing.

"He's not thaaat bad of a dancer! She doesn't see your star power, Major, but I do!"

Major barked happily and started slobbering all over Keys, who started giggling.

"I said star power, Major, not slobber power! Stoooop! It tickles!"

I finished stomping my way up the stairs and flopped onto my bed. It felt like I just kept snapping at everybody. I grabbed my tablet to distract myself. Then I pulled up MyBlock. My whole feed was people doing the Switch Stein Switch. Chris and Crash were learning it. And Auggie was doing it while serving scones at the diner. He was dropping a lot of scones. Chef Scott did not look impressed. And there was that video Carrie said she would post. Frustrated, I logged out of MyBlock and shoved the tablet out of sight. I dropped my face right into the pillow.

"Uuuuuuugh." I let out the biggest groan, trying to feel better. It helped a little. I tried one more, even louder. "Uuuuuuughhhh!" After the second time, I heard a knock on the doorframe. I guess my dad heard all that groaning. He poked his head into the room.

"That's a big ugh, Kar-Star. What's going on?"

I sighed and sat up as Dad came to join me on the bed.

"All anybody is talking about is the Switch Stein Switch! Everywhere I go . . . it's all about that dance," I said.

"Hmm . . . and that's not a good thing?" Dad was confused. Which made sense since I usually wanna shout how great my friends are from the rooftops.

"Well, I wanted to be happy for Switch. She's so cool, and everyone at school should get to see that! But . . . she didn't make up the dance. I did. I did it first and then I showed her the moves and now she's calling it her dance. Just because she added one move. And I know dancing is her thing. But it doesn't feel good."

"Just because dancing is her thing doesn't mean that it's her dance. If someone else made up a rap, you wouldn't say it was yours just because rapping is your thing, would you?"

"No . . . I wouldn't. I'd rather make my own rap. Why didn't Switch just make her own dance?" Talking to Dad always made me feel better.

"Did you try telling Switch how you were feeling?" Dad asked. I nodded.

"Yeah." I paused. "Well, actually I kind of got mad and called her out in front of everyone."

"You must have been feeling pretty hurt to do that."

I nodded. I hadn't *wanted* to blow up on Switch like that. "And then she didn't even really listen to what I had to say. She just got mad. At first, I was just upset about the dance, but now it feels even worse."

"What Switch did, even if she didn't realize it,

was take credit for your work and your creativity. That doesn't feel good at all." Dad squeezed my shoulders, which made me feel the teeniest bit better.

"No, it didn't feel good . . ." My head drooped.

"I'm sorry, Kar-Star. You don't have to be happy for her, and you're allowed to be upset. And I'm so proud of you for trying to stand up for your work. It might have just been one dance this time, but you should always make sure people treat you with respect and know your worth. Especially because this sort of thing happens all the time to Black creators, especially in the music industry!"

"It does?"

"Yes, it does! It can happen in all kinds of ways, big and small. Like an artist not owning the rights to their own music or not being paid for their work. Or like when Black artists don't receive the same attention or success for our music and culture as other people who borrow that culture and pass it off as their own."

"I never knew that. But I guess it doesn't matter now. Everyone already thinks it's Switch's dance."

"It might not seem like it matters in a small way, and maybe that's what Switch thought when she took credit. But what she doesn't realize is all the little ways that taking your success and your work add up. It adds up in the opportunities she gets. Like when Brenda talks about her on TV." That was true. I thought about all the people who had seen Switch's video and thought she had made the dance.

"That's not fair."

"It's not," my dad agreed.

"But . . . I don't want to fight with Switch. She's my bestie. Or at least . . . I think she is." I guess we hadn't talked since our fight. I hoped it hadn't changed things between us.

"You don't need to fight with Switch, but you're allowed to stand up for yourself, your work, and your worth. What you do is up to you, Karma. You should never feel bad about standing up for that. You've got this wonderful, creative, brilliant Karma mind, and it is totally, completely you. And you shouldn't let anyone else take that or make it theirs. There's only one Karma Grant."

My dad always knew exactly what to say. He kissed the top of my head and stood up. He started doing the Switch Stein Switch, but in an extremely Dad-ified way.

"Now, who do you think you got all those smooth dance moves from? It's called the Karma Grant Kick now. But with a little more Conrad Grant flavor!" I had to admit I liked the sound of that new name he had given the dance. The Karma Grant Kick.

When Dad left the room I felt better, but I still didn't know what exactly I should do about Switch. I pulled out my journal and pen and started to write.

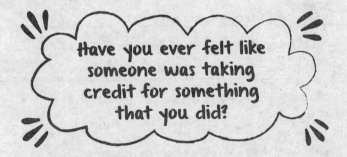

Have you ever felt like someone was taking credit for something that you did?

I tried talking to Switch, but that didn't work. She felt like the dance was hers. But after the conversation with my dad, I'm not so sure I'm okay letting Switch claim the dance. Dad told me there was a lot of history of Black creators having their work taken. I am a Black artist, and I don't want to let anyone else take credit for my work, not even my best friend. I wanted us to do things differently. And I want my work valued. I already tried talking to Switch once! But she doesn't know the history, either. Maybe now that I have this new information to share, things could be different? Maybe we could make a new sort of history. Is it worth giving it a try?

♫ I'm torn up because Switch is my bestie
But this argument is really testing me
She thinks the dance is hers
But I was the one who made those moves first

I'm tempted to give up and let her have it
But I don't wanna let that become a habit
My work has value that she should see
The creativity she's claiming is a part of me

So I can't sit back and let this slide

I wanna change history, starting with my side

I know it's hard, but I know what to do

I gotta stand up, I gotta try talking to you ♪ ♪

I can't just sit back. I have to try again.

CHAPTER 5

The next morning was Saturday. There was no school, so I wouldn't even have to see Switch today if I didn't want to. But part of me wondered if I should just go over to Switch's apartment to try talking to her again. Maybe she was just surprised when I called her out about the dance in the cafeteria. We were besties, and I was sure we could work this out. I *had* to stand up for my work!

I nearly tripped over Keys's scooter on my way downstairs . . . which had definitely gotten bigger over the last few days. It now had even more bells and whistles, and some part of it seemed to be steaming. Was that a frying pan attached to it?

"Keys! Why is your scooter in the middle of the hall?! I almost tripped on this hunk-a-junk!" I yelled in the direction of Keys's room.

I jumped as Keys slid out from underneath the scooter, where he was hard at work with his favorite screwdriver. He was using my skateboard to slide under there like he was a mechanic.

"You almost tripped on the next big innovation in the world of transportation! A scooter that makes scrambled eggs and gets you there in half the time! You'll be walkin' to school and I'll be scootin'! With eggs! And home fries from the Keys Grant patented home fries pocket!" Keys paused and I thought he might be done, but he was just catching his breath. He had a lot to say. "The Scoot-N-Scramble gets you there before you can say—" SQUELCH. Something clearly wasn't right with the Scoot-N-Scramble. It started to rumble, shake, and rattle. Scrambled eggs started to leak out of a canister on the front. With a PLOP, some fell right onto Keys's forehead. Gross!

"Hey! No, it's not supposed to do that. Stop!

Abort! It's an eggsplosion! There's eggs everywheeeeeere!"

There was another satisfying SPLAT. I shook my head at Keys and headed toward the door, leaving him to wrestle with the Scoot-N-Scramble. As I left, I heard Major barking excitedly as he discovered the delicious mess. "Major, do not eat my scooting eggs!"

I walked over to Switch's house and nervously rang the doorbell. I took a deep breath. We barely ever fought, so I was a little nervous, but I knew what I had to say was important. And the longer I stood there, the more sure I was that this was the right thing to do. I knew Switch would understand my side once she heard the history. She loved music and hip-hop as much as I did.

Mrs. Stein answered the door.

"Hi there, Karma!" Mrs. Stein smiled at me.

"Hi, Mrs. Stein! Is Switch here? I was hoping we could talk!" Switch's mom shook her head.

"Oh, no, her dad's already taken her into the studio!" Mrs. Stein smiled like she was telling me something super exciting. Uh. The studio? What was she talking about? Which studio?

"Huh? Which studio?"

"Brenda's studio. You know, it's actually over on the other side of town right near your mom's lab!" That really didn't clear things up for me, but Mrs. Stein must have seen that I was still confused and kept talking.

"Oh, Switch must not have had a chance to tell you! She's going to be on *Good Morning Brenda*'s Saturday-morning show! Oh, it's *so* exciting, I've been calling all my friends to tell them all the good news. She's going to be talking all about that new dance she made! Live!" Mrs. Stein did a little bit of the dance—*my dance*, as she told me the exciting news. Only . . . I wasn't excited. My stomach dropped even farther than I thought it could. I guess there wasn't a misunderstanding. Switch was going to take credit for my dance on *live television*. I felt my eyes begin to water. Mrs. Stein looked at me, a little worried.

"Is everything okay, Karma?" She put a hand on my shoulder.

I just sighed. "Not really, but I think I just need to write in my journal for a little bit." I started to walk home and went through the park. *Good Morning Brenda* started filming in less than an hour. There was no way I could make it all the way across town on foot, and Mom and Dad were both out running errands this morning. There was nothing I could do. Soon Switch would be calling the dance hers . . . on a live broadcast! I walked over to a bench and sat down and pulled out my journal and pen.

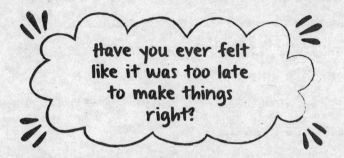

Have you ever felt like it was too late to make things right?

I thought maybe I could help Switch to understand why it wasn't right for her to take credit for my dance alone, but she's about to show the whole city that the dance is hers on live television! I thought I knew what the right thing to do was, but now that I can't talk to Switch, there is nothing I can do but give up. Once she is on Good Morning Brenda . . . pretty much everyone will think the dance is hers. It is just like my dad said yesterday. It is adding up in all the little opportunities she is getting. Is there even anything I can do? Or is it all just too little, too late?

♪♪ Thought I knew the right thing to do

Thought the best move was talking to you

But now it feels like it's just too late

Your decision is made, sealed my fate

But I still want to stand up for what's right

Because my art deserves to see the light

This story has two sides to tell

You're tellin' yours, I gotta tell mine as well

I can't give up, need to talk to you

And I need to tell the world my truth

This dance has been bringin' me so much grief

Only the truth is gonna bring me relief

I finished writing in my journal and I stood up.
I knew what I had to do. I had to find a way to
tell the truth, even if it was just so Switch could
hear it. But first, I was gonna need some help
from Keys.

CHAPTER 6

I ran home and right to Keys's room, which is really more of a laboratory. There was usually a lot of clanking happening in there, and today was no different. The door was shut, but I could hear a loud BZZZZZT. I knocked on the door and heard another BZZZT. And then a CLANK. And then three CLONKs and two PSHHHHs. I thought for sure the noises must have come to a stop then, but then there was a WHIRRRR. And then . . . country music started playing! Followed by a maniacal laugh from Keys.

"Mwahahahaha! We did it, Major! It's aliiiiive!" Major barked excitedly in response. What was going on in there? I knocked again, louder this time.

The door opened a crack, and I could only see the very top of Keys's head and his lab goggles. Through the goggles his eyes looked really big and round. It was like being stared at by a beetle. A *really annoying* beetle.

"Hello, welcome to Keys Grant Enterprises: Inventions and More! Do you have an appointment?" Since when did I have to schedule an appointment to talk to my little brother? I shook my head. Nope, no appointment.

"Hey, Keys, can I come in?"

"Hmm. Maybe later. We're busy!" Keys tried to start closing the door. "Thank you for stopping by Keys Grant Enterprises. Major and I appreciate your— Wait, Major! No, don't!"

But it was too late. Keys couldn't stop Major from pushing right through the door to greet me with some big doggy kisses. I smiled and opened my arms to my slobbery dog. At least *he* had my back! Keys stood in the now open door, and I could see that he was wearing a lab coat and gloves and holding up a large screwdriver.

"Hmph. Please, why don't you come right in." Keys gave Major a look. "I guess my business partner has decided to make an exception even though you don't have an appointment."

Major just lay down and then rolled over, looking for a belly rub. I stepped over the Sammy-Kablammy on the floor, crouched down to rub Major's belly, and looked around Keys's room. There were even more inventions than the last time I had been in here. It was definitely more of a lab than a bedroom. Actually . . . I couldn't even see his bed, it was so buried in inventions. Where did he sleep? In the center of

the lab, there was a big shape covered in some sort of a tarp. It beeped ominously.

"So, how can we help you?" Keys asked. I looked down at Major, who had fallen fast asleep from all the belly rubs. Keys saw this, too, and sighed. "I mean how can *I* help you?"

"Well, Switch is gonna be on *Good Morning Brenda* today," I explained.

"Whoa! That's so cool!"

"Well . . . I mean, I guess it is? But it also isn't.

She's gonna be on *Good Morning Brenda* for a dance that I created. The Switch Stein Switch was mine first."

"Oh. I had only heard that Switch made the dance . . . and it's named after her." Keys looked confused.

"Yeah, because Switch is taking credit for *my* work. And once she's on *Good Morning Brenda*, everyone everywhere is gonna see her doing my dance on television and think that it's hers!"

"So what are you gonna do about it?"

"Well, that's why I came here. I need to talk to Switch and get her to see things from my point of view. I have to stand up for my work. But *Good Morning Brenda* airs live, and it's at eleven on Saturdays!"

At this, Keys and I both looked at the big clock on his wall. It blinked ominously. It read 10:26. It felt like a countdown.

"I need help getting all the way to the

other side of town." I looked at the clock again and gulped. "And fast! Really, really fast."

"Hmm . . . you need to get somewhere . . . and really, really fast." Keys looked around his room while he talked, arms behind his back. He looked at several inventions, considering them carefully. He looked at the Bouncy Ball Blaster and shook his head. He considered the Toilet Paper Helmet 3000 carefully. Finally, he stopped walking and then rushed over to a pile in the corner and started digging through it. He shoved the Colosso-Cleaner to the side, and it made a bur-bling noise and released some bubbles. After a few moments, he held up something that looked like . . . a totally normal helmet. He handed it to me. I looked at it, lifting it up to see if there were any special Keys's features I might have missed. Nope. It was definitely just a regular old helmet.

"A helmet? What do I need that for?" Keys smiled big and turned to the tarp-covered shape in the center of his room.

"I'm so glad you asked! I present to you . . ." With a grand flourish, like when Dad does his magic tricks, Keys pulled the tarp off. ". . . the Scoot-N-Sing!"

It was the new-and-improved version of Keys's electric scooter. It looked like he had decided against the eggs. It had a microphone and—

"Hey! Is that my karaoke machine?"

It looked like the Scoot-N-Sing was half made out of parts from my karaoke machine. There was a spot to input a CD right between the handlebars, which led into a big speaker. Keys ignored me and started to grandly present the many state-of-the-art scooting features. He puffed out his chest, talking like a car salesman.

"You know, after this morning's mishap, I thought it was time to re-scoot, reboot, and change directions. Anyone can make breakfast on the go." I looked at him.

"Did you run out of eggs?"

Keys smiled sheepishly. "Yes, I ran out of eggs, but also not just anybody can bring joy to the people with music on the go! With the Scoot-N-Sing, you can put on a concert anywhere, anytime!"

"Keys, I don't need it to sing. I need it to get me to *Good Morning Brenda* . . . and fast."

Keys smiled. He put a proud hand on the scooter's nearest handle, patting it like a prized pony. "Oh, don't worry, it'll get you there." He pressed a button, and the scooter roared to life. His smile got even bigger as he said, "It has a turbo mode." At the same time, the scooter started blasting a twangy, soulful song.

I don't care if you find me attractive, so long as you find me a tractor / Because loves come and loves go, but one thing I know, still this farm will grooooow.

"Uh, Keys, why is it playing country music?"

"Well, I haven't figured out why yet, but turbo

mode only works when Dad's Nelly Partridge CD is in the karaoke machine." Keys scratched his head while he looked at his own creation.

I took a deep breath. A scooter that only ran on '70s country music? It was gonna be a long ride to *Good Morning Brenda*.

"Good thing I love Nelly Partridge!" Keys said with a smile as he pulled a second helmet out of a pile and plopped it on his head. He started to sing along as he strapped and tightened the helmet. *So long as you find me a tractoooooor!*"

"Wait, you're coming with me?"

"Of course I'm coming with you! Do you think you're gonna learn how to steer this thing in the next fifteen minutes?" He had a point. "Sing it with me, Karma! *Still this farm will groooooow!*" I strapped on my helmet. Keys was a very enthusiastic singer, but he couldn't carry a tune. It was going to be a *really* long ride to *Good Morning Brenda*.

CHAPTER 7

We're on the road and we're going fast! / You won't find a better way to leave the past / When you find that life gets you down / Join me in my l'il buggy, ridin' through the toooooooooown.

"Riding through the tooooown. Sing, Nelly, siiiiing!" Keys belted along with yet another Nelly Partridge tune pouring out of his scooter as we zoomed down the sidewalks of Hansberry Heights toward the studio where *Good Morning*

Brenda was soon going live. I stood on the back of the scooter, with my arms on either side of Keys. I held on tightly to the handlebars. This was not my favorite way to travel. We zigged and zagged along to the beat. We swerved by the diner and surprised Chef Scott so much that he almost dropped his plate of scones.

We passed Ms. Torres in her record shop. Her eyebrows jumped up in surprise. She turned back into the shop and called out. "Winston, look quickly! It's Karma and Keys!" Ms. Torres waved Winston out to see. He popped out of the record shop, and his eyes almost bugged out of his head.

"Whoooooa! Karma, Keys, where you going?"

"Good Moooooorning Brendaaaaaaa!" I called back as we zoomed by him. The wind from our fast approach blew his hair back.

"Good Morning Brenda? Ma, Abuelita, we gotta change the channel!" I laughed as Winston

tripped over himself in his rush to get inside to change the channel on the shop TV set.

"If you get hungry, there should still be some home fries in the front pocket!" Keys shouted over the sound of the music.

I just held on to the handlebars tighter. I didn't want any old scooter home fries. I just wanted to get to the studio as fast as possible. Keys wasn't kidding. This scooter could really scoot. But we were cutting it pretty close on time. Keys must have read my mind because he said, "You knoooow . . . it goes faster if you sing along!"

"Okay . . ." I joined in reluctantly. I didn't really feel like singing—I was more worried about getting to the studio on time, but if it would help, it was worth it! Luckily, my favorite Nelly Partridge song started to play. *Workin' hard or hardly workin', either way somebody's fussin I knooooww!* I joined Keys in belting the chorus: *"I knoooooooooowwww."* Halfway through the chorus, I noticed Keys was shaking with laughter and had tears in his eyes from all his giggling. I stopped singing.

"Keys."

"Yeah, Karma?" He said that way too innocently.

"Does singing along actually make the scooter go faster?" He looked at me with a grin.

"Noooooo. But it does make it a lot more fun!" He jumped back into the song. *"I work long hours, don't get no break."*

I sighed. Then again . . . Keys could be one annoying little brother, but he wasn't wrong. It was a lot of fun to sing and scoot. I giggled at his antics and joined back in.

As we sang, we zipped through the neighborhood, and soon we were nearing the lab where Mom worked as a researcher. We had both been here a few times, so we knew the area. I pointed to Mom's lab when we passed it. "See over there, that's Mom's office, so we should be there soon! Mrs. Stein said it was right near here. I'll keep an eye out!"

Keys nodded and kept steering. Just then, the Scoot-N-Sing started to rattle and shake. We kept zooming, but we started to vibrate.

I shouted to Keys, "Uh . . . Keys, is that supp-p-p-p-os-s-s-s-ed to happen?" This ride had just gotten very bumpy.

"Um . . . not exa-a-a-a-a-c-t-ly!" Keys started pressing buttons to figure out what was going on. The scooter started skipping through Nelly Partridge songs as he pressed the buttons, intermittently making clanks and grinding noises that didn't sound so great. *Workin' hard or hardly workin'*—BZZT—*Join me in my li'l buggy*—CLANK—*Find me a traaaactoooo-o-o-o-o*—BZZT-PSHWOOM. The music started skipping and then fizzled out with more buzzing noises. After that there wasn't any music at all, just clanking and the sound of Keys fiddling with buttons to try and get us running right again. "I think it m-m-m-mi-i-i-ight be overheating!" Uh ... that definitely didn't sound so great. I squeezed tighter to the handlebars as the scooter shook and shuddered.

As Keys tried to keep us scooting, I kept a look out for any sign of the studio. I was so distracted by all the noises coming out of the scooter that I almost missed it. I spotted the building just before we passed it. A giant, glorious smiling billboard with Brenda's face hung over the big gray building.

"Look, Keys! Right there! It's Brenda! This is it!" I exclaimed. Then: "We passed it!"

"Uh ... I'm hitting the brakes!"

But nothing was happening! We weren't slowing down. And now the scooter was CLANKing and GROANing even more. I wasn't nervous about making it to the show on time anymore ... I was more worried about whether we were ever getting off this scooter!

"I got this!" Keys looked determined as he

squeezed the brakes, and the scooter came to a screeching halt. "Lean to the right!"

We both leaned into the skid as we hit the brakes, turning the scooter back around and coming to a slow stop just past the studio. "Whoooooooa, Nelly!"

The scooter shuddered and powered down with a final and resounding CLONK. Keys emotionally patted the handlebars gently. "You did good, Scoot." Phew. I took a minute to catch my

breath, but I didn't have long. I had a show to get to!

"Thank you, Keys. That was some pretty spectacular scooting."

"I know it was," Keys said proudly. "You'd better get in there. It's almost time for the show! I'll try to fix my ride."

I nodded and gave Keys a big hug. As far as annoying little brothers go, I was glad he was mine.

It was time to find my way into the *Good Morning Brenda* studio. I looked up at the billboard. Underneath Brenda's grand smile, it read *Get Ready with Brenda*. I took a deep breath. I *was* ready! Ready to talk to Switch.

CHAPTER 8

Unfortunately, talking to Switch would have to wait just a little longer. Now that I was at the studio, I still had to figure out how to get in. As I rounded the corner and left Keys, I arrived outside the busy *Good Morning Brenda* set. There was a line of people outside the studio excitedly chattering, but I didn't know why they were there.

"Attention! Could I get everyone's attention?

Hi, everybody! Good morning and thank you so much for coming out to be part of our *Good Morning Brenda* studio audience this morning!"

A studio audience? That was exactly what I needed. I kept listening as a man in a white collared shirt with a *Good Morning Brenda* ID card and a clipboard started to organize the crowd.

"Now that you're all lined up, I can tell you a little about what to expect today! I'll be your friendly cruise director, Edwin—"

From the crowd, a confused audience member spoke out. "A cruise director? Are we going on a boat?"

The crowd started murmuring, confused.

"Or are all the audience members getting boats?"

The crowd gasped, excited. Edwin mopped his forehead with a handkerchief and looked a little stressed as he tried to get the crowd to focus again. While he was distracted, I slipped into the line and hoped I looked like I belonged.

"Ahh, no, Pam, no boats." Edwin spoke directly to the confused audience member.

"Oh, good. I get seasick."

"So sorry for the confusion. I call myself your cruise director because I run a tight ship here at *Good Morning Brenda*! That means we will *all* be following the *Good Morning Brenda* rules and protocol. That includes no phones, Ms. Meadows." When he said this, he looked directly at a member of the crowd who had her phone out. He held out his hand. She handed it over. "And *no* food." This time he held out his hand, and she handed over a two-foot-long sub sandwich. Where did that even come from? This Edwin guy was good. Maybe *too* good.

"Now we're almost ready to head into the studio, where I'll need you to walk quickly and quietly to your assigned seats. Remember, there is no wandering during the show. I'll be here to make sure you all get to your correct seats in time for a wonderful morning of getting on top of . . ." Edwin smiled big and waited a second before finishing Brenda's catchphrase, and the crowd eagerly joined him, chanting along.

"EVERYTHING HANSBERRY!"

"Everything Hansberry! Yeah!" I realized what was happening a second too late and quickly tried to say it with everyone else, but I ended up being the only one talking. Oops. I hoped nobody noticed, but Edwin heard my mistimed chant and immediately looked in my direction, narrowing his eyes. He headed straight for me.

"Hi there! I don't think I got a chance to check you in. What was your name?"

"Um . . . I'm Karma." Edwin looked down at his clipboard. Uh-oh. I wasn't gonna be on that list.

"Huh. Doesn't look like I have a Karma on the

list for today's studio audience. Are you sure you booked tickets?" Oh no . . . I hadn't even been here a full minute, and someone was already onto me!

"Did I say 'Karma'? He-he. Maybe you mis-heard me. My name is . . . um . . ."

"Your name is Um?" I was sweating now. Edwin had a really piercing stare, and it was pointed right at me. He could see right through me! I glanced down at the clipboard in his hands and chose a name fast.

"My name isn't Karma, it's, um . . . Carmichael." Edwin looked at me while I tried to remember the rest of the name. Suddenly, the most beautiful music started blasting.

When you find that life gets you down / Join me in my li'l buggy, ridin' through the tooooown. Nelly Partridge to the rescue! It was music to my ears! Keys had gotten the Scoot-N-Sing up and running again just in time. Thank goodness, because while Edwin was looking over at all the noise the invention was making, I took another quick peek down at the list of names on his clipboard. Keys wheeled the scooter by, pausing it right by the crowd and cranking up the volume. Several people in the crowd started murmuring and humming along.

"What is that noise?"

"Is that Nelly Partridge?"

"I love her stuff!"

Edwin huffed. "Excuse me, the scooter parking lot is around the back," he called out to Keys.

"Sorry about that! I was just leaving your fine establishment." Keys winked at me and then started the scooter up again. For once, all that noise was on purpose! My little brother really did have my back! (Even if I *did* have to make an appointment to ask for his help!)

Edwin watched as Keys scootered off into the distance, zigging and zagging through the crowd. I loved Keys as much as he loved Nelly

Partridge! I hoped that Edwin would maybe be so distracted he'd forget he was still waiting for an answer from me.

Nope, no luck. Edwin looked at me closely, waiting for an answer. "You were saying your name?" I quickly remembered the rest of the name I'd seen on the list.

"Right! My name is . . . Rutherford Carmichael." Oops. That sounded like an old man's name. Maybe I should have taken a closer look.

"You're Rutherford Carmichael?"

"Did I say I was Rutherford? Oh, my mistake, sorry, I'm . . . his granddaughter! And I'm here in his place." Phew . . . that was some quick thinking. Edwin narrowed his eyes and looked back down at the list.

"Well, you were late to check in." Edwin tapped his clipboard and looked at me. I quickly apologized.

"I'm so sorry. It was a last-minute change of plans." That wasn't technically a lie. I hadn't been

planning on coming to see *Good Morning Brenda* today.

"Hmm . . . well. Miss . . . Carmichael, follow the line and take your seat." Yes! Perfect. I joined the line and started walking. toward the studio doors. I'd be in the studio in no time, and then I'd be able to talk face-to-face with Switch before she took credit for the dance. This was gonna be a breeze.

CHAPTER 9

This was not a breeze. I thought it would be easy to get to Switch once I got into the studio, but I was wrong. Edwin the usher made sure we all made it to our seats, and then he went up onto the stage to explain our role as audience members.

"Hello, everybody! Now remember, your biggest job as members of the *Good Morning Brenda* audience is to do whatever this sign says!" It was a big neon sign. To show us how it worked, Edwin clicked through the two options. "APPLAUSE—when this one is on, we'd love to see you clapping! ON AIR—when that one goes on we need you to make sure you're not talking! Take it easy for now … in just a few minutes Brenda will be here!" Edwin switched it to APPLAUSE, and the crowd cheered excitedly. I had to admit, I was pretty excited to see Brenda live. But I reminded myself that I was here for a reason. I had to find Switch.

Of course, finding Switch was easier said than done. Once Edwin was done explaining, he started to patrol the aisles, keeping a close  eye on all of us. I watched him collect another three cell phones, a tablet, a bag of pickle chips … and at least two more sub sandwiches. Where were all these sandwiches coming from?!

"Aaaachoo!" Pam sneezed from the row in front of me, and before I even had a chance to say "Gesundheit," Edwin was already there to shush her and hand her a tissue! He had been all the way on the other side of the audience! How did he even do that? Brenda might have been on top of everything Hansberry, but Edwin was on top of everything *Good Morning Brenda*!

I was seated near the back of the studio audience. Excited Brenda fans filled the rows in front of me, all the way down to the big *Good Morning Brenda* stage I saw on my TV. There was her chair and the chair for the guest. That's where Switch was gonna sit. But where was Switch now? And could I find a way to talk to her?

I was in an aisle seat—it should be easy to sneak out and find her. I craned my neck, looking all around for Switch. Brenda wasn't on the stage yet. There was just a lot of people prepping cameras and equipment for the show. I tapped my foot nervously. I needed to get to

Switch *before* the show started. I looked both ways, keeping an eye out for Edwin. No sign of him. I needed to make my move . . . now. I stood up and started to turn . . . and bumped right into Edwin.

"Ahem."

How did he move that quickly and quietly? Edwin moved as quietly as Dad when he was trying to open the pickle chips without Major and Keys finding out! (They always found out— they had super hearing when it came to pickle chips.)

"Heeeey, Edwin!" I turned to look at him and tried to sound excited to see him. I was not. He had his arms crossed and his clipboard in hand, and he definitely did not look excited to see me. I guess the feeling was mutual.

"Did you need something, Miss Carmichael?" Edwin whispered.

"Miss . . . Carmichael?" I was confused until I remembered that was what I told him my name was. I guess I wasn't all that sneaky. I wouldn't be a very good spy. "Oh, right, Miss Carmichael! That's me! Well, I just thought I'd run to the bathroom before Brenda gets started. Don't wanna have to go when I'm trying to get on top of everything Hansberry, you know."

"Hmm. Well, the time to use the restroom was before check-in. The show is actually about to start, so we do ask that you keep your seat until after we film, as we are about to be a live studio. The ON AIR sign is going to be on shortly and I'm afraid I can't let you back in after that."

Ugh, getting locked out of the show would not help me find Switch. I sighed and sadly dropped back into my chair.

After all that . . . I wasn't going to see Switch before the show. Maybe this whole mission was a waste of my time. I wasn't going to get to talk to her and try to explain my side of the story again. And instead I'd just have to watch her do my dance . . . on television!

Suddenly, there was a hush, and then the clack of a pair of shoes. The crowd started to cheer loudly. Brenda was walking out onstage. It was time!

 ACTION!

CHAPTER 10

A hush fell over the crowd again as Brenda approached her chair. As always, she was in a blazer and a skirt. Her shoes clacked loudly on the stage, echoing through the crowd. The crowd that had just been excited about a prize was completely silent. Brenda was definitely a star. This was her stage, and she knew it. She was a Hansberry icon! She finished crossing the stage and smiled at the crowd once she reached her chair.

"Hello, hello! And welcome to *Good Morning Brenda*! Thank you so much for coming out to join us today! I hope your audience experience has been a good one so far. Has Edwin been taking it easy on you?" She paused to smile at Edwin, and then laughed. "Just kidding, Edwin doesn't take it easy! That's what we love about him. Hope none of you have ended up on his bad side!" At this I gulped. I might have ended up on his bad side. Brenda looked out at the directors and producers waiting by the cameras.

"Well, it looks like we're about to get this show started! Are you ready?" The audience cheered again. Everyone here was ready to see Brenda do her thing.

A producer spoke up. "We're live in three, two, one . . ."

The director made a sign with her hands, and the ON AIR sign clicked on. I held my breath. I wasn't going to be making a peep. The last thing I needed was Edwin on my case again.

"GOOD MORNING, HANSBERRY!" Brenda's voice boomed as she greeted the audience watching on their TVs all across the city. "Are you ready to get on top of . . . ?" Brenda looked at the audience expectantly and waited for us to finish, just like Edwin had outside. This time I was ready!

"EVERYTHING HANSBERRY!" I joined the audience in shouting. It was actually kind of cool to be in the audience for my mom's favorite TV show. Maybe I could still have fun even if I had lost my chance to talk to Switch. Then this morning didn't have to be a total bummer. From that moment on, I was the perfect audience member, the kind who would have made Edwin proud. I applauded when the APPLAUSE sign lit up. I said, "Awwww," when Brenda put a picture of a baby sloth on the screen behind her. And I listened carefully to all the Hansberry news that Brenda was covering.

"Now, this morning, we have a very special guest here at *Good Morning Brenda*. I'm sure many of you have seen her doing her thing on MyBlock." This was it . . . Brenda was about to bring out Switch as her guest. "I tried learning some of her moves on my own. A little clap here, and a little roll there." Brenda did a few small dance moves—my dance moves—from her chair, and the audience laughed. She joined in the laughter and added, "I guess I should leave the dancing to the experts! And that's exactly what we're gonna do! Here today to show us how to do the Switch Stein Switch . . . please put your hands together for this morning's guest, local Hansberry dance sensation . . . SWITCH STEIN!" I joined the audience in clapping, but my heart wasn't in it like it was for that baby sloth. I was not excited for this part of the show.

Switch walked out from the side of the stage. She seemed nervous, but she waved to the audience and then went to sit down on the sofa

opposite Brenda. This was the first time I had seen Switch since our argument in the cafeteria. I was still hurt and still wanted to stand up for myself, but I wasn't as angry as I had been before.

"Good morning, Switch! Thank you for joining us!"

"Good morning, Brenda!" Switch greeted her brightly.

Brenda smiled. "That's the name of our

show . . . don't wear it out!" The audience laughed. Brenda made that joke almost every episode.

"Thank you so much for having me on today!" Switch seemed really nervous. I knew she wasn't that used to the spotlight, but she didn't usually have stage fright.

"Of course! I had to have the amazing dancer behind the Switch Stein Switch on my show!"

My stomach dropped. There it was. Switch was the dancer behind the Switch Stein Switch. I looked away, but before I did, Switch looked a little uncomfortable. Why was she so uncomfortable onstage? She danced in front of people all the time. Maybe it was just because she had to talk on camera.

"Now, this dance has quite a few moves. And we all know I could use the help, so at the end of our show today, we're going to have

Switch walk us through the moves of her dance. Doesn't that sound exciting?"

The audience roared in response. Wow, they really did all love the dance. And none of them knew it had anything to do with me. They didn't even know I existed. And that was because of Switch.

Brenda kept going. "But first . . . we have a surprise announcement for Switch as a thank-you for coming on."

My eyes widened. A surprise announcement?

"We here at *Good Morning Brenda* love to support the arts in our community's youth. It's not that long ago that I was Little Brenda, editor of the Peach Tree Middle School newspaper. And look at me now! So, it is our great *Good Morning Brenda* honor to announce that to help her become the best dancer, choreographer, and producer she can be, we will be sponsoring Switch's attendance at this spring's Camp Rhyme!"

CHAPTER 11

I gasped. Brenda was sending Switch to *the* Camp Rhyme. The audience started cheering before the APPLAUSE sign even went on. They were all so excited for Switch. But I couldn't bring myself to join in. I looked down at my hands. I didn't want to see Edwin and the sign reminding me that I was supposed to applaud again, and I definitely didn't want to see how excited Switch was. I didn't want to clap for this. It wasn't fair. And it was exactly what my dad had said would happen. Switch had taken credit for my dance, and now it was adding up into all these new opportunities. That camp was *my* dream. I needed to find a way to go, to become the best rapper I could be. And now Switch was just gonna *get* to go all because she hadn't told people I made up the dance. I couldn't believe it.

Brenda waited for the crowd to quiet down and then smiled. "I KNOW! Isn't it soooo exciting. We'll talk to Switch about Camp Rhyme and more, after 'Brunch with Brenda'! But first, why don't we head on over to my kitchen!"

As Brenda moved over to the in-studio counterspace to start her usual cooking segment, I finally looked up. Why didn't Switch look excited? I couldn't understand it. If I had been told I was getting to go to the *coolest* camp in the world, I would have been smiling so big you could see it in space!

Any kid who loved hip-hop like me and Switch would do anything to go to that camp.

Brenda was making frittatas, and the audience was loving it. But frittatas were the last thing on my mind. I pulled out my journal and hoped Edwin didn't notice. I just really needed to write out how I was feeling.

Have you ever been really disappointed in a friend?

I want to put the dance behind me and focus on enjoying the show, but all I can think about is Switch taking my spot at my dream camp. I'm not sure if I'm more disappointed that Switch is going to the camp of my dreams because of a dance that I made up, or that she took credit for my dance to begin with. Both make me feel really bad. And even though I've tried really hard, I haven't been able to get to Switch before the show and tell her how I feel about her taking my work. It feels like there is nothing else I can do. Everyone thinks the dance is Switch's now. Maybe I just have to smile and applaud when the sign tells me to.

♫ Switch has been taking credit for my dance

And now Switch is gonna take my chances

Thought she was the kind of person who stood

up for a friend

But maybe I was wrong . . . maybe this is the end

But it can't be, I don't want it to go down like this

I gotta explain all the opportunities I'll miss

She has to know the privilege and the history

Maybe she'll admit there's more to this story

It isn't right to take credit for someone else's art

We can change the story, this can be the start

I gotta know my worth and stand up for my creativity

That's the only way we can make this right to me ♪ ♪

I don't know if my friendship with Switch can be the same after this. But I still have to try and stand up for myself. Just like Dad said. I know the worth of my work, and I have to tell her that.

The sound of applause brought me out of my journal. Brenda had just finished making her frittata, and the APPLAUSE sign was blinking bright red. That frittata did look delicious. "Yum! That's all our time for 'Brunch with Brenda' . . . and now let's go to commercial! And when we're back . . . we'll learn the Switch Stein Switch with Switch Stein herself!"

CHAPTER 12

By the time the ON AIR sign had clicked off for the commercial break, I had made up my mind. I had come here for a reason, and even if I couldn't talk to Switch before the show, there was no reason I couldn't tell her how I felt *during* the show. Brenda was headed backstage. Switch was sitting alone onstage, fiddling with something in her hands. This commercial break was my chance. I could slip away, get to Switch, and tell her how all this made me feel before the show came back. But the walk from my row to the stage was long, and there was no way I'd make it without Edwin stopping me. He wouldn't even let me go to the bathroom. There was no chance he was gonna let me near Brenda's stage.

I just needed a little distraction to keep Edwin from spotting me. I wished Keys and the Scoot-N-Sing were here to help me out again. Think, Karma, think. I started looking all around for something to distract Edwin with. But no luck. I even poked my head under my chair. I must have bumped into the seat in front of me. Pam and her family turned around and saw me poking out from under there.

"Is there something under our seats?"

"Uh—" There wasn't anything under my seat, but suddenly I realized . . . maybe I didn't have to make a distraction. Maybe other people could distract Edwin for me.

"What's going on?"

"Did I hear there were gifts under the seats?"

"I didn't know there were going to be gifts!"

"Gifts?"

"Is it a car?"

"I heard it was a Jet Ski!"

Suddenly, whispers were traveling from one person in the audience to the next. It was like a giant game of telephone, and I could hear the ideas getting sillier and sillier as they passed between rows until the audience was just a low, excited hum.

"Jet Ski?"

"Paragliding lessons?"

"A date to the movies with Brenda?" The rumor spread through that crowd faster than Mr. Singal and his turtle in the three-legged race on Peach Tree Middle School Field Day. (Cuebert can really move when he wants to!)

⭐ ‖ ⭐

I looked back at Edwin, and he was once again mopping his forehead with his handkerchief as he tried to get the crowd to quiet down. "Excuse me, everyone, please keep quiet. We'll be back on the air shortly!" But he was losing control of the crowd. They were too excited about the possibility of *Good Morning Brenda*–branded Jet Skis! This was my chance! While he tried to tell people that there was no prize waiting for us after the show, I slipped out of my seat and made a beeline for the stage.

I made my way down the stairs toward the stage. I stayed low and tried to look as inconspicuous as possible. Maybe nobody would see me. Switch was still not really looking up at the crowd. I wonder what had her distracted. Maybe she was reading about all the cool things she'd get to do at Camp Rhyme. I heard they had rap battles in canoes.

I was almost there. I was one row away. I got right up in front of the stage and I was about to call out Switch's name when I ran right into someone. Someone in a white shirt, holding a clipboard. Aw man.

CHAPTER 13

I knew who it was before I looked up. After all that . . . Edwin had still managed to stop me. Where had he even come from? I had to admit, he *was* really good at his job, but it was kinda getting in the way of my plan. I had to talk to Switch and explain how I felt. And now I was finally just one row away from Switch, but Edwin was in my way. I looked up.

He did not look happy. "Miss Carm—"

Switch looked up quickly when she heard the first half of my alias, but she hadn't spotted us yet. "Karm—did someone say Karma?" Switch glanced around.

Edwin did not seem to hear Switch and kept talking. "Miss Carmichael—"

Switch looked disappointed as she heard the rest of the name and went back to looking at her lap.

"I'm going to have to ask you to return to your seat immediately. As I explained before, you must stay seated for the duration of the broadcast." Edwin really was a stickler.

Switch ignored him and continued to focus on something in her lap. In spite of Edwin's instructions, I didn't move. I still had to talk to her! But I was frozen. I hadn't talked to Switch since our argument. For the first time since getting here, I was a little nervous about how she would react when she saw me. I had been so focused on getting to talk to her that I hadn't stopped for long enough to let myself think about how it would go. She didn't know I was going to be here, and I definitely wasn't *supposed* to be here! She was going to think that I had come to ruin it for her.

"Miss Carmichael, if you do not return to your seat, I will have to escort you from the studio and ask you to wait outside until we are off air."

Oh man, I was really in it now. Switch looked up to see who was getting in trouble, and this time, she saw me. And she broke out in the biggest, most excited smile. Huh? That definitely wasn't the reaction I was expecting.

"Okay, Miss Carmichael, we will be leaving now."

I sighed and started to turn to follow Edwin. I had a feeling I was not going to be welcome back at *Good Morning Brenda* in the future.

"Miss Carmichael? Huh? Karma?!" Switch looked very confused when she heard what Edwin called me. I giggled even though I was in big trouble. That name was going to be a hard one to explain.

"Miss Stein, is there something you needed from Miss Carmichael? Maybe you can catch up after the show, as she was *just* leaving." Edwin tried to direct me toward the exit, but I ducked around him.

"Wait! I need to talk to Switch!"

At the same time, Switch stood up from her chair. "Wait! Stop! She's my best friend." She, literally, stood up for me. Even with all the dance trouble, it warmed my heart to see my bestie try to help me out.

Edwin stopped. He did not look like he was going to budge. "Please, Miss Stein. I have to follow our *Good Morning Brenda* protocol. No audience members can be out of their seats. It's in the handbook."

"Edwin, pleeeease? I've been trying to talk to Switch all day. That's why I came all the way across town."

Switch looked touched, but Edwin did not.

Then something amazing happened. I didn't even realize that the whole crowd was watching us. They started to chant, "Let them talk! Let them talk!" Edwin looked very annoyed.

Pam stood up. "Edwin, they're like Brenda and her best friend, Mikaela! Nothing can come between them!"

The crowd murmured in agreement. Pam was right. Brenda did love friendship. She talked about it *all* the time. For the first time, Edwin seemed to soften. Not very much, but just the slightest bit. More audience members started to speak up.

"She came all this way. That's beautiful!"

"Brenda loves friendship!"

"Brenda does love friendship. And so do I," Edwin said, nodding as he came to a decision. The crowd held their breath. "Fine. Miss Carmichael, you may have a few minutes with Miss Stein. But, Miss Stein, I expect you back onstage before we come back from commercial." Switch came running to the front of the stage and hugged me. The crowd cheered excitedly, ignoring the fact that the APPLAUSE sign was still off.

"Thank you, thank you, thank you, Edwin!" I could have hugged him, too, but I didn't know if thank-you hugs were *Good Morning Brenda* protocol. I gave him a high five, and he smiled. Maybe deep down he was a softie after all! Really deep down. I turned back to Switch. She started talking fast, like she had been thinking about what she had to say for a while, too.

"Karma, I'm so sorry I didn't listen to you yesterday. You were upset and you're my friend, and I should have taken that seriously."

"I accept your apology, but I still have something I need to say." I was about to tell Switch everything I had come here to say, when we heard a voice.

"This is even better than *Good Morning Brenda*!" It was someone from the crowd. Oh . . . we still had an audience. We turned to look at the crowd, who were all still watching us.

Switch giggled. "Maybe it would be more private backstage."

"Yeah," I agreed.

We slipped out of the studio to the more quiet backstage area. It hadn't even been a full day since our argument in the cafeteria, but it had felt way longer. I had learned a lot since then, too. I took a big breath and prepared myself. This was gonna be sooo hard, but I had to say it. Even though we were besties. Actually, I had to be honest with her *because* we were besties, and I wanted us to stay that way. "Switch, I still don't think it's right that you took credit for *my* dance. That's my work and my creativity. You *are* a really great dancer, and you made it so fun! And your beat is amazing—I wouldn't have come up with the dance without it! But I still came up with the dance, and you didn't acknowledge that when you posted it on MyBlock."

Switch stayed quiet. Maybe she didn't want to hear what I had to say. But there was more.

"And my dad told me all the ways people have been taking credit for Black people's art and work for years. Especially in the music industry. And even though I *know* you didn't mean to. I had to tell you that and tell you that my work matters." I took a deep breath and said the most important part, just like I had said with Dad and written in my journal. "I have to stand up for my work and my worth. It's not fair for you to take credit for my dance and get to go to Camp Rhyme."

"You're right, Karma."

Uh . . . what? That was not what I expected at all. I thought Switch would be mad like she was yesterday.

"You agree?"

"Yeah. It was your dance first, and I shouldn't have taken credit. And even if I didn't realize I was taking credit at first, you're my bestie, and I should have listened to you when you told me something upset you. So I'm double sorry."

I was confused. "But you're on *Good Morning Brenda* to talk about the dance."

Switch nodded. "It all happened so fast this

morning—we rushed here before I had a chance to tell you. I've been trying to reach you on MyBlock all day to try and talk to you before I went on the show!" I furrowed my eyebrows. Huh? Messages?

"I was even messaging you during commercials!" Switch held up her phone. *That's* what she was looking at in her lap.

"But I didn't get any messages!" Then I remembered pushing my tablet to the side yesterday afternoon. Oh. "Oh . . . actually . . . I logged out of MyBlock yesterday because I was so tired of seeing everyone talk about that dance!"

Switch nodded. The whole time I was trying to talk to Switch . . . she was trying to talk to me. I got a warm feeling inside. We really were besties, and together we could get through anything.

"What were you trying to message me about?"

"I wanted to tell you how sorry I was. And that I wanted to make it right."

I thought about what my dad had said. How was she planning on making that right? The whole city thought it was her dance.

"Make it right?" I asked.

Switch smiled big.

"I came up with an idea last night. But I think it'll be even better with you here."

CHAPTER 14

This time I watched from backstage as the ON AIR light flicked on. Brenda and Switch were in their seats again.

"Welcome back to *GOOD MORNING BRENDA!*" The audience cheered as Brenda got the show rolling again. "Before we wrap up this morning's show, we have here Switch Stein to show us the steps to Hansberry's hottest dance craze!"

Switch braced herself, and then spoke up. "Actually, Brenda, I don't think I should be the one to show you the dance."

Brenda looked completely shocked, and the audience looked confused. "Huh. And why wouldn't I have Switch Stein show me the Switch Stein Switch?"

Switch stood up, bravely facing the audience and the cameras. "Because I took credit for inventing the dance. It was my friend Karma's dance first, and I added to it. That dance is actually called the Karma Grant Kick, not the Switch Stein Switch."

I felt lighter already hearing Switch call the dance by the new name. Everyone watching *Good Morning Brenda* all across Hansberry finally knew the truth.

"Karma Grant came up with the dance that everyone loves. And she should be the one to show it to you. And most importantly, she should be the one to go Camp Rhyme."

I knew now that Switch had been so nervous onstage because she had been planning to tell the truth all along.

Brenda's eyes were wide, but she recovered quickly and took back over. "I have to say, this is a first here at *Good Morning Brenda*. But I do love a surprise guest! Come on out . . . KARMA GRANT!" I walked out onto the stage. The audience burst into applause again. I looked out into the crowd—it was hard to see anyone past the bright lights shining on the stage and the cameras pointed at us, but I thought I could just make out Edwin mouthing the name Karma Grant in confusion. I'd always be Miss Carmichael to him. "So, Karma . . . will you show us the dance?"

I nodded. "I'd love to."

Someone cued Switch's beat, and it started to play. This time I wasn't annoyed to hear it at all. In fact, it was just as much fun as the first time.

As the beat started, I smiled and started to do my original moves. I went through it the same way I had with Switch just a couple days before. "First, you cross your fists across your body like you're hitting your hips." Brenda stood up to follow along. "And then when this part of the song comes, you want to sliiiiide!" Brenda and I slid across the stage together. "And then you clap above your right leg, then you lift your leg and clap under it this time."

Brenda had trouble with this part and almost lost her balance. "Whooooaaa! Whew, Karma has me workin'!"

The audience laughed. They were loving it.

"And then you spiiiiiiiiin and do a shoulder roll like this!" Brenda did the roll. "And then you end with Switch's extra-special Arm Swing Thing!" I dropped to the ground, and Brenda followed, dropping clumsily to the ground. I gave Switch a thumbs-up. "And that's it! You did it!"

Brenda jumped up and took a bow. The

audience cheered. I smiled and turned to see where Switch was. She had crept off backstage.

Brenda addressed the audience, gesturing for them to get up and out of their seats. "Okay! Time for all of you to get up and moving and learn the dance. Karma, can you show them again?" I could show them again . . . but I could think of one way that would make it better.

"Sure! But you know, I wouldn't be able to do this dance without my bestie Switch's *fire* beat. Do you think she could come help us teach everybody?" Brenda liked the sound of that.

"That sounds like a great idea to me. After all, I do need all the help I can get. Wouldn't want to embarrass myself on live TV!" Hearing Brenda, and seeing me wave her out, Switch came out to join our dance. She took her place on the other side of me, so I was in the middle facing the crowd.

"Let's hear that bumpin' beat again!" Brenda signaled for Switch's beat to start playing again,

and the three of us started doing the dance. The audience tried to follow along, having a blast. Even Edwin was doing it! And he wasn't half-bad!

Dancing up there with my bestie, showing the world our moves, I felt like I was on top of the world. I started rapping before I could help myself. Switch's beat was perfect for dropping a quick rhyme. *"Karma and Switch showing* you our moves / We know our worth, so we can't lose / Cross your fists and slide real slick / Now you're doing the Karma Grant Kick / Give it a remix, change the sitch / Swing your arm out, that's the Switch Stein Switch."

The audience didn't need the APPLAUSE sign this time. They were out of their seats cheering when Switch and I finished doing our dances to my new rhymes. Brenda was impressed. She glanced at the studio clock.

"My goodness. We're out of time. This has certainly been a *Good Morning Brenda* to remember! Thank you all for watching, and for getting on top of . . ." As always, Brenda waited to finish her closing line with us. We all joined in.

"EVERYTHING HANSBERRY!"

"Now I think I have a phone call to make. I can't see why *Good Morning Brenda* can't send two aspiring young musicians to Camp Rhyme." Switch and I looked at each other, eyes wide, realizing what that meant. We couldn't believe it. When the ON AIR light finally clicked off, we both jumped up and down, next level excited.

"Wait . . . that means . . . we're going to Camp Rhyme . . ." We both shouted the next part out loud.

"TOGETHER!"

I gave Switch the biggest hug. She started excitedly listing all the things she had heard about Camp Rhyme.

"I heard there's Beatboxing Bonfires and a start-of-camp Rhyme Off and an end-of-camp Hip-Hop Hoedown . . . and I heard there's s'mores!"

"That all sounds completely and totally amazing. But I'm most excited that I'll get to do it all with my bestie!"

Switch nodded in agreement. "Yeah, it's gonna be totally next level!"

We were going to have the world's best spring break. All of a sudden, Switch's phone

started going off just like it had yesterday. PING—PING—PING. Messages were coming in nonstop again. Switch looked at her phone and smiled big. I didn't say anything. She must have been getting a lot of new comments on the Switch Stein Switch because of our TV appearance. I couldn't change everything that had happened the past couple of days, even if we did make it right.

"Uh, Karma, you should take a look at this!" She held up her phone. It wasn't the Switch Stein Switch video at all. It was a new video. Winston had *already* uploaded a video of our appearance onto MyBlock. I guess he had gotten his mom and Abuelita to change the channel after all.

I read the title out loud to myself. "'Karma Grant debuts the Karma Grant Kick'!"

Comments were rolling in from all our friends and family and people from all over Hansberry. They loved the dance, and they loved our performance. I couldn't believe it. Crash, Chris, Sabiya, and Megan and all the other neighbors who had been so hype about the Switch Stein Switch were now giving me my shine. I had to admit, it felt pretty nice.

Switch and I started walking out of the studio, arms around each other. Switch just had one more question. "Hey, why did that grumpy guy keep calling you Miss Carmichael?"

I giggled again. "It's a really long story."